ALICE McLERRAN

Dreamsong

Pictures
by VALERY VASILIEV

Tambourine Books
New York

For Sophie, and my own three. A.M.
To the memory of my mummy and daddy. V. V.

Inquiries should be addressed to Tambourine Books,
a division of William Morrow & Company, Inc.,
1350 Avenue of the Americas, New York, New York 10019.
Printed in the United States of America

Library of Congress Cataloging in Publication Data

McLerran, Alice, 1933- Dreamsong/by Alice McLerran; illustrated by Valery Vasiliev. p. cm.
Summary: A boy searches fields, forests, and mountain for the song he hears
each night in his dream, unaware that the true source is in his own home.
[1. Songs—Fiction. 2. Bedtime—Fiction.] I. Vasiliev, Valery, ill. II. Title.
PZ7.M47872Dr 1992 [E]—dc20 91-32622 CIP AC
ISBN 0-688-10105-4 (trade) —ISBN 0-688-10106-2 (lib.)

1 3 5 7 9 10 8 6 4 2
FIRST EDITION

In a village so far away from the here and now that people still ate porridge for breakfast and not everyone had forgotten how to do magic, there lived a boy named Pavel. For as long as Pavel could remember, every night he had dreamed a dream in which he was listening to a wonderful song. Yet no matter how many times he heard that song in his dreams, when he awoke it was gone.

Early one morning as he sat at the breakfast table, he was trying so hard to remember his dreamsong that he quite forgot to eat his porridge. His mother was puzzled to see him just sitting there with his spoon in the air, humming this note, humming that note. "What is it, Pavel?" she asked.

"Why can't I think of how my dreamsong goes?" he exclaimed. "If just once I could hear it when I'm awake, I know I could remember it! There must be *some* way I could hear it."

Pavel's mother and father looked at one another, and then smiled at him. "If it is so beautiful," said his father, "then perhaps you should go look for it. But if you think you must travel far to find it, let me help you." He reached out his arms, lifted his son onto his lap, and stroked Pavel's bare feet. "As long as the sun shines today, you can run and climb as far and as fast as you choose, and you won't feel tired."

Pavel felt a tingling in his feet, and he knew that magic was working.

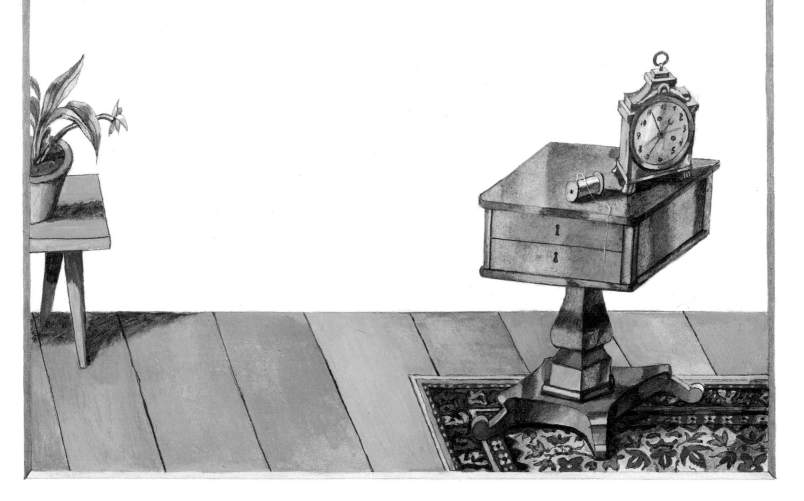

"If you must travel far, you'll get hungry," said Pavel's mother. And while Pavel dressed, she took a pack and filled it with good things to eat. "Now," she said, helping him fasten the pack upon his back, "go in search of your dreamsong—but remember, come home before the sun goes down!" And she kissed the back of his head.

Pavel ran through the village, ran through the meadows, ran into fields and forests far from any he knew. The sun was already climbing high into the sky when he heard ahead of him the song of a river singing to itself on its way to the sea. It was his dreamsong! In the center of the river the water rushed along joyously, singing:

Loveliness without an end!
Ah, what lies around the bend?

But at the edges of the river, ripples lingered against the mossy banks softly, wistfully. The song they whispered was different:

Loveliness that is today,
Loveliness that cannot stay. . . .
Rivers flow into the sea,
Gliding into memory.

"But that's nearly the end of the song!" thought Pavel. "There's a lot more that comes before *that*. Maybe the beginning of the song is at the beginning of the river."

So Pavel followed the river upstream, up into the forests covering a great mountain. Up and up he followed it, clambering over granite boulders, climbing slopes so steep that he had to pull himself up by grasping at rocks and roots and branches.

At last, when the sun was already overhead, the slopes began to grow more gentle, and forest opened into meadow. What below had been a river was here only a stream wandering quietly through the grass. In the center of the meadow grazed a small flock of sheep watched over by a young shepherd boy. The boy welcomed Pavel with a smile and led him over to where two pails were cooling in a shallow curve of the stream. One was filled with fresh milk, the other with wild blueberries.

Pavel suddenly realized how hungry he was, and brought out some of his own lunch from the pack. The two boys quietly shared their food as the young lambs frisked and grazed nearby.

As soon as they had finished eating, the shepherd picked up his flute and began to play. A familiar song curved through the air, reaching out to caress the lambs, brushing tenderly across their soft heads. Pavel hugged his knees, wanting to laugh with pleasure. He knew what the flute was singing:

> Sweet the grass and warm the sun,
> Learn to leap and dance and run.
> Nothing in the world to fear—
> If you need me, I am near.

That was his dreamsong, all right—but just the middle part. He still needed to find the beginning, and the sun was starting on its way down toward the horizon. As the shepherd continued playing, Pavel waved good-bye and continued on uphill.

As he neared the top of the mountain he began to hear a new sort of music, rippling notes that mounted triumphantly from warm deep tones to silvery high ones. Following the sound, he

came to a little cottage next to a spring. He had reached the source of the river — and surely that melody was the very begin- ning of his dreamsong!

Entering the open door of the cottage, he found an old harpmaker seated at a shining new harp. The harpmaker nodded a welcome; the music never paused. The harp was singing the song that was in the old man's heart:

> All the beauty that I knew,
> All the love, I put in you.
> Now the music can take wing;
> Now the song is yours to sing.

Without taking his eyes from the harp, Pavel sat down. It was nearly suppertime; he held out the last of his food to the old man. The harpmaker smiled, shook his head, and continued playing. Surrounded by that wonderful music, Pavel himself forgot to eat. The rays of the sun stretched longer and longer across the room.

All at once, Pavel realized that the light within the room was tinged with rose. The sun was setting! Quickly he threw on his pack, waved good-bye, and ran outside. Down the mountainside he flew, so swiftly that forests and meadows streaked past his vision like streams of sunset clouds. Never, never had he run so fast. He reached his house at the very moment the sun sank behind the mountains.

His mother and father were standing at the door waiting for him, and Pavel ran into their arms.

"Did you find your dreamsong?" his mother asked.

"Yes, but not all at once," he answered. "Part here, part there. The last part first, the first part last. Maybe not quite all of it—I don't know. Anyway, what I found was wonderful . . . but oh, all of a sudden I'm so *tired*!"

His parents helped him into his nightclothes. Then Pavel's father rocked him in his arms while Pavel's mother tied on her apron and fixed him a cup of warm milk. As Pavel finished the milk, cradled in his father's arms, his mother began to sing the song she sang to him each night at bedtime. Always, every night, she sang that song to him. It was a wonderful song—triumphant and tender, joyous and wistful. But Pavel, this night as always, was fast asleep so soon that he heard it . . . only in his dreams.

All the beauty that I knew,
All the love, I put in you.
Now the music can take wing;
Now the song is yours to sing.

Sweet the grass and warm the sun,
Learn to leap and dance and run.
Nothing in the world to fear—
If you need me, I am near.

Loveliness without an end!
Ah, what lies around the bend?
Loveliness that is today,
Loveliness that cannot stay. . . .

Rivers flow into the sea,
Gliding into memory.
Gliding off, and born again—
Rain to river, sea to rain.